Planet Kayterus

The Flying Orange

A Black Hole

The Space Giant's Beanstalk

Oddball

Major Tom

Series 814

The Fun Guys Stories:

The Spring Time and the Moth Ball
The Hen Coat and the Ship Shape
The Rat Race and the Sky Lark
The Bottleneck and the Mole Hole
The Mush Rooms and the Fox Glove
The Mouse Trap and the Cricket Team

The Adventures of Major Tom:

The Planet of the Elves
The Missing Ambassador
The Space Pirates

First edition

© LADYBIRD BOOKS LTD MCMLXXXII

Adventures of Major Tom
The Planet of the Elves

written and illustrated by PETER LONGDEN

Ladybird Books Loughborough

The flying orange hurtled
through space passing stars
and planets as it patrolled
the galaxy. Inside were
Major Tom and his robot
partner, Oddball, ready
and waiting for their
next mission.

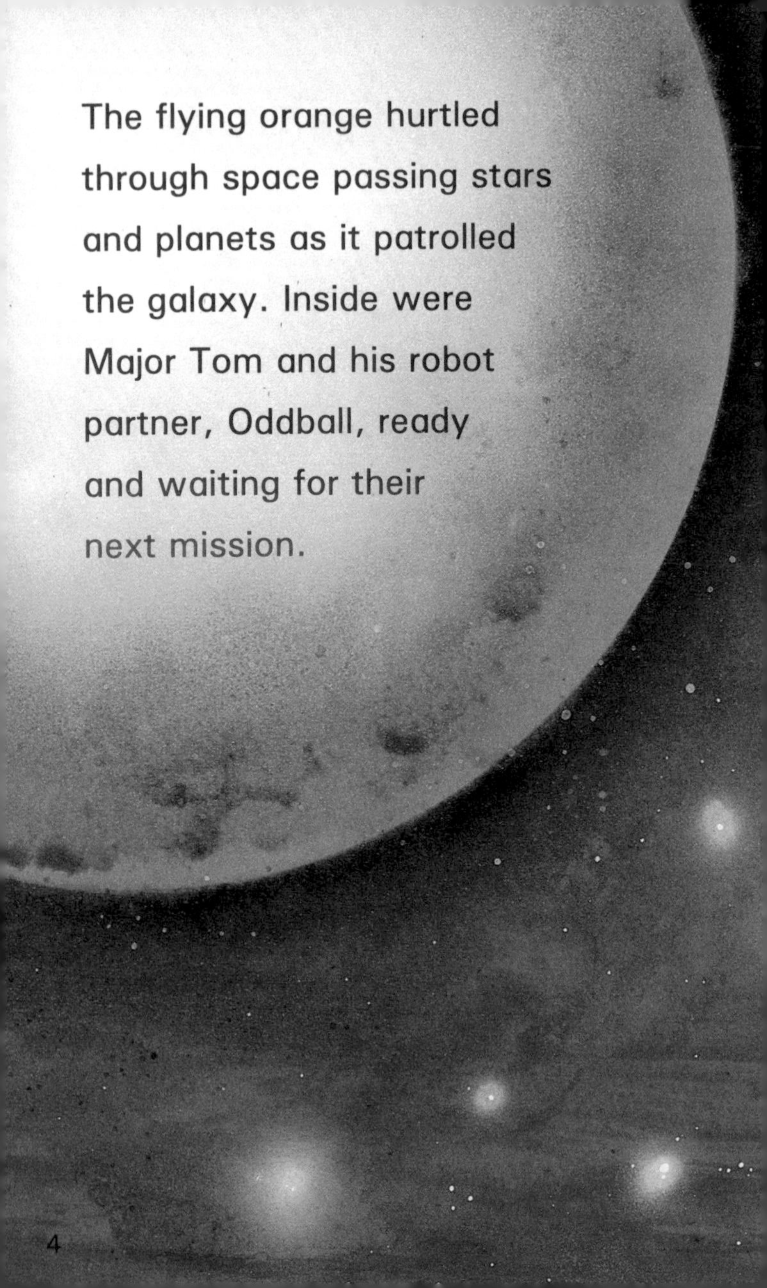

Everything was very quiet inside their spacecraft. In fact Tom and Oddball hadn't had an adventure for quite a while.

They had just filled up with fuel at a friendly planet and while Oddball checked over the engine, Tom was taking a short nap.

The orange flew on through space until suddenly the peace and quiet was shattered by the loud bleeping noise of the interplanet telephone. This telephone kept Major Tom in touch with base control on Earth.

"I knew this quiet life wouldn't last for ever, Oddball," said Tom. "Base control must have a new job for us."

Tom put on the headphones and said, "This is Major Tom. Come in, base control!" After a moment of crackling on the line Tom heard the voice of base control, loud and clear . . .

MAJOR TOM — GO IMMEDIATELY TO THE MOON — THE CHEESY MOUNTAINS ARE DISAPPEARING — YOUR MISSION IS TO FIND OUT WHAT IS HAPPENING AND STOP IT — BASE CONTROL OUT!

Tom took off the headphones. He looked puzzled and worried. What could be wrong on the moon, he wondered.

"Oddball! Set a course for the moon. Full speed ahead! There isn't a moment to lose," ordered Tom.

The orange swung on to its new course.

9

As the flying orange zoomed through space getting nearer and nearer to the moon, Tom told Oddball about base control's orders.

Soon they could see the moon ahead. Oddball shouted, "Get ready for landing!"

They fastened their seat belts and they landed with a gentle bump on the moon's surface.

Tom and Oddball looked out. "You stay with the orange, Oddball," said Tom. "I'll go out and take a look."

Tom opened the hatch and stepped out on to the moon. His nose twitched as he smelt the mountains of cheese all round him.

Tom decided to keep out of sight until
he knew just what was happening.

"This is strange," thought Tom, as he
peeped over a chunk of cheese.

"What is a mushroom doing here on
the moon?" Tom wondered if he
should go back and fetch Oddball.

Suddenly he was surrounded by a crowd of little green elves. They began loading pieces of cheese into the mushroom.

"It's time to find out what's going on," he muttered to himself. He grabbed one of the elves. "Now who are you and what is that mushroom doing here?" demanded Tom. The elf began to explain how their planet had been invaded by a fierce space bandit, the Hooded Rat.

"There are green elves and red elves there but the red elves have gone over to the Rat's side. They are making us take huge amounts of cheese from the moon in that mushroom spaceship," finished the elf.

"Well, we're here to help and there's no time to lose," said Tom. "Off you go and Oddball and I will follow."

They left one green elf as a guide for Tom and these two waited until the huge mushroom spaceship had taken off.

"Come on," urged Tom. "Let's get back to the orange."

The orange went at top speed to catch up with the mushroom. Tom told Oddball what had happened as they travelled along the Milky Way.

Inside the orange the little green elf was very worried. He told Tom about all the dangers which they might find on the planet now that the Hooded Rat had taken over.

"Don't worry," said Tom. "You're safe in the hands of one of Earth's most famous space patrols."

But just as he spoke, Oddball shouted, "What's this heading towards us?" As they looked through the porthole they could see a large, ugly object travelling straight towards the orange.

"Oh no!" yelled the terrified elf. "It's Astro-squid. He flies around in space waiting to eat tasty looking space-ships."

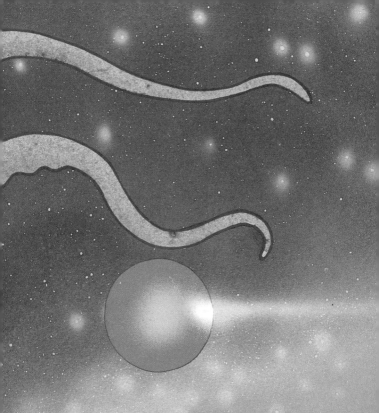

The space squid's long tentacles began
to wrap themselves around the orange.
He'd been flying round for hours looking
for a bite to eat.

The squid laughed and began to
squeeze.

23

"Action stations!" shouted Tom and he leapt to the controls of the laser gun. Taking careful aim, Tom fired a blast of pips straight into the enemy's eyes.

"It's a hit! Well done, Major!" yelled an excited Oddball.

Slowly they began to feel the squid releasing its terrifying grip on the orange. As soon as they were free Tom altered course and steered the orange away.

At last their journey was over and the orange arrived at the planet of the elves. As they orbited the planet, looking for a place to land, they spotted one of the Hooded Rat's red elves on guard patrol.

It was too late. The red elf had spotted them.

The scout wasted no time in reporting to the Hooded Rat. The evil looking rat rubbed his hands in glee at the thought of blasting the flying orange into outer space.

"Shoot as soon as they come into firing range!" he snapped at the red elves.

Aboard the flying orange, Oddball was worried. "We're getting too close, Major!" he shouted.

"Reverse thrust! Stop engines!" ordered Tom. "I've got an idea."

The flying orange halted in mid air and hovered. Below, the red elves were confused. ''Quickly!'' said Tom. ''Launch Segment One. This will fool them.''

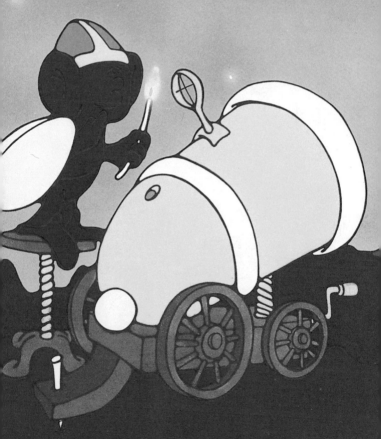

Tom was right. The red elves could not believe their eyes as Segment One, the orange's high speed mini-ship, peeled away from the orange and shot off at high speed.

"They are escaping!" cried the furious Hooded Rat.

Now that they were out of danger, Tom, Oddball and the elf guide made their way to see the Green Elf King.

''We'll collect the flying orange later,'' said Tom, as he parked Segment One and they all got out.

The planet was beautiful and Tom and Oddball forgot about the dangers as they moved on up the hill to the palace.

Inside the palace, the little elf introduced Tom and Oddball to his king. He explained how famous they were, and told the king that they would get rid of the Hooded Rat, once and for all.

"Fine, fine!" said the king. "What's the plan?"

"The plan?" said the little elf, looking puzzled. "Have we got a plan, Major Tom?"

"A plan?" repeated Tom. "Of course we have a plan! Come along, Oddball, we have work to do."

So the Major and Oddball left the king and went away to think about what they should do next. In the end it was Tom who came up with a splendid idea.

Tom's plan was to bait a huge trap with the biggest, smelliest piece of cheese on the planet.

This would tempt the Hooded Rat out of his castle and down to the cheese — one bite, and the trap would be sprung.

"And that," said Tom, "will be the end of the rat. Any questions, Oddball?"

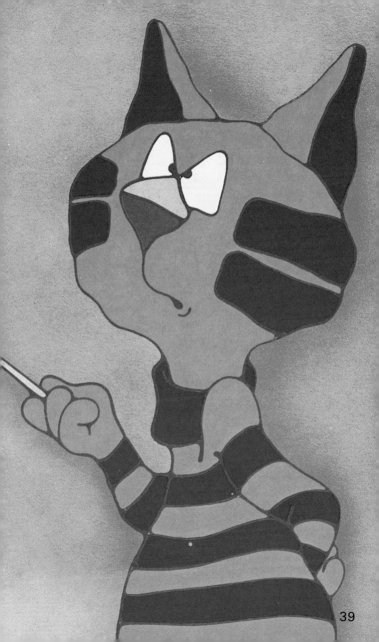

At the back of the palace, Oddball set to work.

The green elves helped to collect all the bits and pieces they would need to build the giant trap.

Tom yawned and settled down to watch. After all, it was his idea so he couldn't be expected to make the trap as well.

By nightfall the trap was finished, with the smelliest piece of cheese in the kingdom in position on it.

Now came the difficult job of taking the trap to the Hooded Rat's castle.

It took hours for Tom and Oddball to pull and push and pull a bit more, as the trap inched its way up the hill to the castle. They had to keep a constant lookout for any red elf guards but they saw none.

By the time they got to the castle Oddball was exhausted. It seemed to him that the Major had given a lot of orders but he hadn't done much pushing!

At last the trap was in place. Then Tom whispered, ''You go over there, Oddball, while I set the trap.'' Oddball followed his orders, and was joined by some green elves who wanted to watch.

''Keep very quiet, everybody,'' said Tom, struggling with the steel spring. ''Phew — this cheese *is* ripe! **Ah-ah-atchoo!**''

There was a tremendous SNAP! Tom was in the trap himself. "Well, at least it works!" said Tom, waiting to be set free.

Then — "Too late!" yelled Oddball. "Here comes the Hooded Rat!"

"Well, well, well! What have we here?" snarled the evil looking rat.

"I'm Major Tom of the Space Federation," came the reply, "and I'm arresting you!"

The Hooded Rat sneered. "You're in no position to arrest anybody. You are my prisoner."

Then Oddball sprang to the attack.

With his metal arms and legs swinging,
Oddball hurled himself at the Rat.

His extending arms clawed at the rat's
face, and then — it happened. The face
came away! It was a mask, and
underneath was a simple rat who
wouldn't frighten anyone.

The elves cheered as they realised they
had been tricked and their planet was
no longer in danger.

Later that night they sent the rat off into outer space in his own spaceship. Once he had gone, the red and green elves made friends again. They were happy to think that they would never see the rat again.

But it would be a long time before Tom
wanted to see another piece of cheese.

SS Moon Cheese

Pisces

Little Bear

A Magnetic Field

Great Bear